Radiance:

The Passion of Marie Curie

by Alan Alda

SAMUEL FRENCH

FOUNDED 1830

SAMUELFRENCH.COM

ISBN 978-0-573-70060-6   Printed in U.S.A.   #20354

MUSIC USE NOTE

Licensees are solely responsible for obtaining formal written permission from copyright owners to use copyrighted music in the performance of this play and are strongly cautioned to do so. If no such permission is obtained by the licensee, then the licensee must use only original music that the licensee owns and controls. Licensees are solely responsible and liable for all music clearances and shall indemnify the copyright owners of the play and their licensing agent, Samuel French, Inc., against any costs, expenses, losses and liabilities arising from the use of music by licensees.

IMPORTANT BILLING AND CREDIT REQUIREMENTS

All producers of *RADIANCE: THE PASSION OF MARIE CURIE must* give credit to the Author of the Play in all programs distributed in connection with performances of the Play, and in all instances in which the title of the Play appears for the purposes of advertising, publicizing or otherwise exploiting the Play and/or a production. The name of the Author *must* appear on a separate line on which no other name appears, immediately following the title and *must* appear in size of type not less than fifty percent of the size of the title type.

RADIANCE: THE PASSION OF MARIE CURIE was first presented by the Geffen Playhouse, under artistic director Randall Arney and managing director Ken Novice, at the Audrey Skirball Kenis Theater in Los Angeles, California; with scenic design by Tom Lynch, lighting design by Daniel Ionazzi, sound design by Jon Gottlieb, costume design by Rita Ryack, projection design by John Boesche, and production stage management by Young Ji. The director was Daniel Sullivan. The cast was as follows:

ÉMILE	Hugo Armstrong
PIERRE	John de Lancie
PAUL	Dan Donohue
MARIE	Anna Gunn
TERBOUGIE/TORNEBLADH	Leonard Kelly-Young
MARGUERITE	Natacha Roi
JEANNE	Sarah Zimmerman

CHARACTERS

ÉMILE

PIERRE

PAUL

MARIE

TERBOUGIE/TORNEBLADH

MARGUERITE

JEANNE

TIME

For the most part, the play is set between 1898 and 1911.

SET

The actors in the company will be seated on a bare stage, taking in the action of the play. When their turn comes to play a scene, they will frankly rise, meet downstage and play it.

Images suggesting various locations are projected on the upstage wall.

The only furniture is a set of straight-backed chairs and occasionally a bed and a small table, all brought into play by the actors.

(The actors enter. Some take their seats, while some move props. **ÉMILE BOREL** *moves a chair as he speaks to us.)*

ÉMILE. In Paris, at 10 Rue Vauquelin – out back, behind some ancient buildings – you'll find a makeshift laboratory, a crumbling shed. Stifling in the summer, freezing in winter – with a few pine tables that were once used to dissect cadavers. Could there be a more ideal place for a couple to spend the happiest days of their lives? How could you not love this miserable old...

(SLIDE: MARIE AND PIERRE'S LAB)

PIERRE. *(overlapping)* ...This miserable old shed. Rain blowing in through broken panes in the ceiling – the old stove belching a layer of dust onto our experiments... *(blowing dust off the table)* We hate it and we love it.

*(**MARIE** turns to **PIERRE**. She speaks with a slight Polish accent.)*

MARIE. Pierre...

PIERRE. Yes?

MARIE. Don't laugh.

PIERRE. At what?

MARIE. I'm wondering...I might have a...

(She stops herself.)

PIERRE. A what?

MARIE. No. I don't know.

PIERRE. Marie, what is it?

MARIE. Why did Becquerel stop?

PIERRE. Why did he *stop?*

MARIE. He found those strange rays coming out of uranium and then he just dropped it. He didn't even measure them. I don't understand him. Isn't he curious?

7

PIERRE. So, what are you thinking?

MARIE. What if I did that for my thesis!? What if I measure the rays coming out of uranium. Is that valuable enough for a thesis?

PIERRE. Yes! Of course it is.

MARIE. But, is it original enough? It's just a measurement...

PIERRE. But, nobody's done it. Do it.

MARIE. I could use your electrometer. And the piezoelectric balance. I put a weight on the quartz and when it gives off a charge, I compare that charge to the charge...

PIERRE. You compare that to the charge coming off the uranium – yes. And when the charges balance, you've got it!

MARIE. What do you think?

PIERRE. Do it. It's perfect.

MARIE. It is, isn't it? *(delighted, kissing him quickly)* Every time I add a weight to the quartz, the charge goes up by a discrete amount. I'll get absolute pre...

(He kisses her, lingering on her lips. She comes up for air.)

...Precision. You're so greedy.

(She kisses him again, playfully.)

PIERRE. So are you.

MARIE. *(taking his hands in hers)* Do you know how lucky I am? To have you?

PIERRE. Not as lucky as I am.

MARIE. No. Much much *much* luckier. You give me courage. You want me to want what I want.

PIERRE. Of course I do.

MARIE. You see? You have no idea. You think *every* man would want me to want what I want?

(MARIE kisses PIERRE's hand. PIERRE offers his eyes for a kiss. She kisses them. PAUL enters and stops when he sees them.)

PAUL. *(smiling)* I might have come at an awkward moment. Should I come back?

PIERRE. No, that's all right, most moments are like this. What are you up to? Take a chair.

PAUL. This is very exciting. I think this could work. I'm really sorry to barge in on you like this.

PIERRE. No, no. Tell us.

PAUL. I'm putting gas phase ions in a weak electric field. If I'm lucky, I'll actually be able to determine the velocities of individual ions!

PIERRE. Excellent!

PAUL. Now, *that* would be interesting, wouldn't it!

MARIE. Absolutely beautiful.

PIERRE. Excellent!!

   (SLIDE: ÉMILE'S STUDY AT HOME)

ÉMILE. They're both very encouraging, aren't they?

   (PAUL turns to ÉMILE.)

PAUL. They sit there with me until late at night and let me go on and on about ionizing gases. Then they come up with these penetrating questions. And she's...Marie is just...they're like one brain. They finish each others thoughts. There's something touching about that, don't you think?

   (ÉMILE is writing a formula on his blackboard as they talk.)

ÉMILE. Yes, well, I wish they would take a break from physics once a day. They talk physics while they *eat,* for God's sake.

MARGUERITE. *(entering with a dish)* You're supposed to be eating *lunch* now. He does that, he gets up in the middle of a meal and comes in here and scribbles. Can I get you some cake?

PAUL. No. I'll just watch Émile scribble for a while, then I have to get back to the lab.

MARGUERITE. *(putting down the dish)* Don't forget to eat. ...
Hello.

ÉMILE. What...?

MARGUERITE. Don't forget to eat.

ÉMILE. Didn't I just eat?

> (**MARGUERITE** *looks at* **PAUL** *as if to say, cheerfully, this is what I live with. She exits.*)

PAUL. *(to* **ÉMILE***)* Can I ask you a favor? Please say no, if you can't do it.

ÉMILE. Of course, what?

PAUL. If I gave you 800 francs, could you hold it for me? I want to give it to my mother, but I won't see her until the end of the month.

ÉMILE. And you'd like me to hold the money until then?

PAUL. If it's inconvenient I completely understand.

ÉMILE. No, not at all. But, why don't you just keep it in a drawer?

PAUL. At home...

ÉMILE. Yes.

PAUL. I can't do that. It wouldn't be safe. Jeanne would find it.

ÉMILE. Jeanne. *(beat)* Your wife.

PAUL. Yes.

ÉMILE. Well, of course. I'm happy to hold it for you.

> (**PAUL** *takes the money out of his hatband and counts it.*)

Why didn't you ask Pierre? They'd be glad to hold this for you. They love you.

PAUL. I can't. I couldn't stand the look in Marie's eyes if I thought she was disappointed in me. The problem is I worship her.

ÉMILE. You admire her. We all do.

PAUL. No, I worship her. Don't ever say I said that. Please. Not even to Marguerite.

(ÉMILE *returns to the blackboard and hums Beethoven's* Ode to Joy.)

I hope I haven't made you uncomfortable.

ÉMILE. Why would you think I'm uncomfortable?

PAUL. Because when you're uncomfortable you tend to start humming Beethoven. Émile, please don't judge me.

ÉMILE. No, no...

PAUL. I can't help it. She's amazing. So infinitely curious. And *precise*. She keeps notebooks, diaries...about everything in her life...

MARIE. *(at her journal)* Irene is born. Three kilograms... One bottle of champagne to celebrate the baby: three francs. Chemist and nurse: Seventy-one, fifty.

PAUL. *Nothing* escapes her attention. *Nothing.*

MARIE. Irene now weighs 3.2 kilograms *before* nursing. 3.3 kilograms *after* nursing.

PAUL. How could you not fall in love with someone who's both obsessed and meticulous?

(SLIDE: MARIE AND PIERRE'S LAB)

(MARIE *is at her apparatus. She has carefully placed a weight on the balance and read the result.)*

MARIE. *(confused, agitated)* Pierre! I need you.

PIERRE. *(entering)* What? Are you all right?

MARIE. This is giving off rays!

PIERRE. What is?

MARIE. *(rattled)* I wanted to see if anything else gives off rays. Besides uranium. I've been trying gold, silver, all kinds of things. I was just curious.

PIERRE. So?

MARIE. Why are the rays coming out of pitchblende?

PIERRE. You put pitchblende in there?

MARIE. Yes, why are rays coming out of it?

PIERRE. Well, pitchblende has uranium in it, so of course it gives off...

MARIE. No. This is from that place in Bohemia. They took all the uranium out when they mined it. This is just slag now, but it's still giving off radiation.

PIERRE. So, maybe there's a little residue of uranium in there.

MARIE. No, Pierre, listen. *(holding up a canister)* This is uranium. *(holding a small rock)* This is pitchblende, after the uranium has been taken out. It's just slag. This slag is twice as active as pure uranium.

PIERRE. No.

MARIE. It's crazy. We have to get more of this. You think they'd give us some?

PIERRE. It's just lying there on the ground. I'll ask them.

MARIE. Beg them. We have to study it. Even if they send us just a little.

(A chute opens on the back wall and slag starts to spill out. [Note: an alternative effect is to have a sliding door open on the back wall as the slag piles up, filling the doorway behind a wire mesh. Later in the play, the door can be closed.] MARIE and PIERRE turn and watch the slag pour onto the floor. It keeps coming.)

PIERRE. *(finally)* That's quite a bit.

MARIE. That's the *first* truckload. There are twenty more.

(MARIE shovels the slag into a large pot. It's heavy. [The actual pot weighed 20 kilos.] She lugs the pot to a fire and stirs it with a rod that is as long as she is tall. Steam rises from the pot.)

PAUL. *(entering, observing her)* I came by and watched you work today – stirring pots of pitchblende. Boiling it down. Boiling down the residue, then the residue of that. I can't tell you how it moves me when sweat gleams on that pale skin that I can only steal a glance at. When concentration creases that brow that I'll never be able to kiss. It broke my heart, watching you place a weight on a bit of quartz to measure its charge. You did it with the lightest, most delicate touch – a touch I'll never be able to feel.

(MARIE, at her apparatus, carefully balances a small weight on the dish of the balance.)

MARIE. ...Pierre! Look at this! *(almost alarmed)* I precipitated it with ammonium...

PIERRE. Yes...?

MARIE. Now it's four hundred times more active than uranium! *Four hundred.*

(They are stunned, almost as though this were a catastrophe.)

PIERRE. *(in a hushed tone)* My God. If there's no uranium at all in that slag...

MARIE. ...Then, what's giving off all this radiation?

PIERRE. ...There could be a new element in there.

MARIE. Let's not get ahead of ourselves. There's a lot more slag to go through.

PIERRE. *(glancing at the enormous pile of slag)* Yes...yes!

MARIE. Irene now weighs 9.2 kilograms; the circumference of her head is 44.3 centimeters...

(lighting change)

The substance we have extracted from pitchblende contains an element never before known. We're calling it Polonium – after the name of the country of origin of one of us.

(lighting change)

...I took 3.6 Kilograms of fruit and the same weight in crystallized sugar. I boiled it for ten minutes and passed it through a fine sieve. I got fourteen pots of very good gooseberry jelly...

(lighting change)

This is extraordinary: We think we have a *second* new element! Pierre took it to Demarçay for spectral analysis. If the existence of this metal is confirmed we propose to call it radium.

PIERRE. Demarçay couldn't believe it. He said, "My God, what is this?" I said, "Whatever it is, it's 900 times more radioactive than uranium." He got a clear spectral line. It doesn't correspond to any known element.

(They hug. PAUL enters.)

PAUL. It's true...You did it, didn't you?

MARIE. We found it, yes!

PAUL. *(hugging PIERRE)* I heard from Becquerel.

MARIE. We've definitely got it.

PAUL. This is fantastic. You must be thrilled.

PIERRE. You can't imagine. And I can finally get back to crystals.

MARIE. Well, we still have to isolate it.

PIERRE. Actually isolate it?

MARIE. Well, yes.

PIERRE. You want to keep going?

MARIE. Why wouldn't we?

PIERRE. She's amazing. We've spent two years on this. You're exhausted.

MARIE. We can't stop now. There's a new element in there.

PIERRE. You actually want to keep going on this.

MARIE. I don't see my children from morning until night. It's painful to me, sometimes it's unbearable... but, all right, I can live with that. I can get freezing eyelids and bleeding fingers. What I *can't* do is stand by and let someone else isolate radium.

PIERRE. But, that's just about who gets the credit.

MARIE. Pierre, no...

PIERRE. Really, that's all it is... That's not worth ruining your health over. You're exhausted. What's the matter?

MARIE. Never mind. It's childish of me.

PAUL. What is?

MARIE. Never mind, forget it.

PIERRE. Marie, what is it?

MARIE. It's like going back to Szczuki.

PIERRE. It isn't.

MARIE. I can't go through that again.

PIERRE. You won't. It's not the same thing.

MARIE. It is!

PAUL. I'm sorry, what are you talking about?

MARIE. Szczuki.

PAUL. What's shookie?

PIERRE. It's a town in Poland.

MARIE. A very small, very provincial town.

PAUL. Why can't you go back there?

MARIE. No, I don't mean literally. I was eighteen. I was desperate to get an education…God, this sounds idiotic. Forget it.

PAUL. Please, tell me.

MARIE. First of all, you're a child in school and you're not allowed to learn your own language. It's Russian or nothing. Your father and mother's language doesn't exist. How does that make you feel?

PAUL. It must make you feel terrible…

MARIE. It makes you feel like *nothing*. But that's not good enough for the Russians. If you're a woman, your education stops dead at the door to the university. You can't even study in *their* language! So now, you're *less* than nothing. I had to go to *Paris* to study! And that's how I wound up in Szczuki.

PAUL. I'm sorry, I don't think I follow that.

PIERRE. You don't have to follow it, this is really directed at me.

MARIE. *(to PIERRE)* It *is*. I had no money. I couldn't *afford* to move to Paris. So, I go to that pitiful little town – Szczuki – to work as a governess.

PIERRE. …Marie, I know.

MARIE. *(to both PAUL and PIERRE)* I have to be constantly available to this petty, pretentious family for everything, even when they need a fourth for bridge, which is extremely boring. Then, one day the family's son comes home from a trip and we fall in love. And the family goes crazy. Don't be ridiculous, you can't love a *governess*. She's nothing. And they put me on a train. That did it. As the train pulled out of town, I promised myself...I *promised* myself, Pierre...I will not disappear into nothingness. And I won't. I can't. So, that's my sad story. Maybe it's weak of me, but, Pierre, please, please understand.

PIERRE. No, I do understand. *(beat)* I'll put crystals aside for a while...

MARIE. I'm not asking you to do that...

PIERRE. ...I'll get back to them later.

MARIE. I don't expect you to stop working on...

PIERRE. You can't do this alone. There's too much of that stuff to sift through.

PAUL. How much radium is *in* all that slag? Do you actually know?

PIERRE. No idea. Maybe only one part in a hundred.

PAUL. That could take months.

PIERRE. I guess it could.

PAUL. *(seeing* **PIERRE** *struggle to get out of his chair)* You know, you're more exhausted than Marie. Look at you.

PIERRE. No, no, no. That's just a little arthritis. *(to* **MARIE***)* Come on, we'll have some fun. We'll hold hands and jump in there together. We'll stuff our nostrils with foul chemicals until we choke. We'll cover ourselves with the muddy slime of ten tons of slag.

MARIE. *(touched)* That's the most beautiful thing any man has ever said to a woman.

*(***PAUL*** exits.)*

PIERRE. *(to the audience)* But it isn't one part in a hundred. It's one in a million. It doesn't take months, it takes *years* of digging, boiling, testing.

(SLIDE: SAME LAB – A DIFFERENT CORNER OF IT)

MARIE. Are you in pain?

PIERRE. No. Not even if I press right where I put the radium.

(PAUL *enters.*)

PAUL. Am I too late?

MARIE. No, we're just taking the bandage off.

PIERRE. *(rolling up his sleeve)* You want to see? Come here. I put a tiny bit of radium on my skin for ten hours 21 days ago. Look.

(PIERRE *shows them his arm.*)

MARIE. *(delighted)* It's a burn! It's a definite burn! Look at the *size* of it – six square centimeters!

PIERRE. At first it was just kind of red, and now *this*.

MARIE. It's a real wound! Look, it's oozing! Isn't that amazing?

PAUL. *(trying call up some enthusiasm)* Yes. Very nice.

MARIE. Deep mortification. Fantastic! Pierre, this is thrilling.

(SLIDE: MARIE AND PIERRE'S GARDEN)

(MARGUERITE *enters with a tray of drinks, along with* PAUL, JEANNE, MARGUERITE *and* ÉMILE.)

JEANNE. Marie, are you crazy? You can't be serious with this.

PIERRE. Jeanne, the radiation destroys tissue.

MARIE. It can probably kill cancer cells.

(taking the tray from MARGUERITE*)*

Thank you.

MARGUERITE. You actually put it on your skin? What happened?

PAUL. Suppurating sores.

PIERRE. It's beautiful.

ÉMILE. You know, I hate to say it, but this sounds dangerous.

MARIE. Émile, be honest. If you could prove a mathematical theorem by burning your skin with it, you wouldn't do it?

ÉMILE. Didn't Pierre put mice in a closed space with radium?

MARIE. Yes.

ÉMILE. And what happened?

MARIE. They died. What point are you trying to make?

ÉMILE. You handle it, you suck it up into pipettes – I've seen you do that! Why are you fooling with radiation?

MARIE. Why are we *fooling* with it?! Because when uranium gives off enough radiation, it turns into *a whole other element!* There's something going on inside the atom. It's giving up something and changing into something else. The atom may not be the smallest thing in the universe! My God, Émile, we walk around, surrounded by this mysterious fog of the unknown. And all we have to do is step into the mystery. Isn't that worth a little risk?

JEANNE. Well, it's nice to know those things but, my God, it sounds like you're playing with fire.

PAUL. Jeanne. This is science. It's not "nice" to know these things. It's monumental. I'll explain it to you when we get home.

JEANNE. Oh please, she's wearing herself out. Look at those circles under her eyes. She's starting to look haggard!

PAUL. Jeanne!

JEANNE. Well, look at her. No wonder she gets morose.

PIERRE. She doesn't get morose.

JEANNE. Let's be frank. We love Marie – but you can't go around dressed in black, smelling poison gases all day and not get a little *morose*. Am I right? Aren't those fumes poisonous?

PIERRE. Well, if you were to inhale them directly. So, we always try to work outside, but then it snows, and we have to move back inside. It smells awful.

JEANNE. But, you have to use really toxic chemicals, don't you?

PIERRE. Yes, because the radium is all bound up with barium and we have to separate it out with fractional crystallization.

JEANNE. *(totally mystified)* Fractional *what?*

PAUL. That's a little technical for Jeanne. *(to JEANNE, casually condescending)* But, intuitively, you hit on something. Good for you!

JEANNE. *(resenting his tone)* Yes. Thank you... Anyway, it's making you morose. I'll bet any amount of money the last time you wore something other than black was on your wedding day.

PIERRE. *(lighting his pipe)* You're right. She wore navy. She was lovely, too.

MARIE. Dark colors are practical. I spend my whole day cooking up pots of mud.

JEANNE. That's what I wear an apron for.

PAUL. *(lightly, joking)* Cooking up pots of mud?

JEANNE. *Meaning?*

PAUL. *(innocently, playfully)* Meaning?

JEANNE. I don't understand that remark. If you want Châteaubriand, Professor, then bring home something monetary I can take to the butcher.

PAUL. Jeanne, I was teasing.

JEANNE. There might be more interesting things on your plate if you didn't spend your time researching things that don't exist.

PAUL. Mathematical objects do exist.

JEANNE. There. "Mathematical objects." How in the name of God can an idea be an object? It defies common sense. I know you all think I'm a philistine, but why do scientists have to be so obsessed? Walking around with their head in the clouds... *(to PAUL, with some malice)* Here's an idea: Try coming home with a few francs in your pocket. That might bring you down to where the rest of us are.

PAUL. A few minutes ago there was a woman in your chair who was only slightly acidic. Where did she go, I wonder?

JEANNE. Where did *you* go? That's the question.

(The air in the garden is getting very heavy. ÉMILE *eases the tension by breaking into a few bars of Beethoven's* Ode to Joy.*)*

(Light change: Evening in the garden.)

(The friends move off. MARIE *cleans up.* PIERRE *takes out a letter.)*

MARIE. Jeanne was outrageous today.

PIERRE. *(after a slight beat, nodding)* She's insulting.

MARIE. She has that streak of anger in her.

(when PIERRE *doesn't answer)*

You know? Are you all right?

PIERRE. *(holding up a letter)* I couldn't tell you while they were all here. This came in the mail from Mittag-Leffler. They've decided to award the Nobel Prize for our work on radiation.

MARIE. Pierre! I thought something terrible had happened. *(beat, realizing)* It has, hasn't it?

PIERRE. First of all, the prize will be just for the work on *radiation*. Not for the discovery of radium. They won't believe we have a new element until they can see it.

MARIE. I thought so. It's not good enough that we got it down to a salt. I knew it.

PIERRE. They want the pure metal. Pure radium in a dish.

MARIE. Of course.

PIERRE. There's sort of a vague hint that there might be a prize some day for whoever comes up with that. But they'll have to be able to *see* it.

MARIE. All right. So, it's just for radiation. That's better than nothing.

PIERRE. Marie – they want to present it to me and to Becquerel. But not to you.

MARIE. *(after a beat)* Well, that's a surprise, isn't it.

PIERRE. It's infuriating. Why would they do this?

MARIE. They're afraid of giving the prize to a governess. *(beat)* How did this happen? Do you know?

PIERRE. The French Academy sent a nomination to Stockholm. It completely ignored what you did.

MARIE. We should talk to Lippmann. And Poincaré.

PIERRE. Why?

MARIE. Because they were my mentors. We can ask them to object to the nomination.

PIERRE. Lippmann and Poincaré both put their names to it.

MARIE. *(stung)* Very nice. Something lacking in them as mentors, wouldn't you say?

PIERRE. They just can't conceive that a woman could have done this. They can't conceive of it.

MARIE. They can. They just won't. Well, damn them. They can go to hell!

PIERRE. I can't accept this without you. I'll write to them. Maybe I can sway them.

MARIE. But, what will you say?

PIERRE. I don't know, I can't tell them they're bigots.

MARIE. So, then…?

PIERRE. Well – we did this together – they should give it to both of us…because…

MARIE. Yes…?

PIERRE. …Because it's more aesthetically pleasing that way. It's symmetrical.

MARIE. That seems to lack a certain amount of…actual meaning.

PIERRE. Yes, but it's hard to argue with, isn't it?

(SLIDE: ON THE TRAIN, SWEDISH COUNTRY-SIDE WHIZZING BY)

(Sound: the rumble of a train)

(MARIE, sitting next to PIERRE, is writing on a post-card. She reads it to PIERRE.)

MARIE. My Darling Irene. So much excitement! We're on our way to Stockholm. Two whole days on the train. You'd love it. We hate it.

(smiling at PIERRE, who doesn't respond)

I'm very proud of your daddy. He wrote a brilliant letter to the Nobel Committee and they had to give in. *(to PIERRE)* Why do you suppose they gave in? I thought that letter you wrote was very peculiar. Pierre, speak. You haven't said anything since Belgium.

(PIERRE looks at her unhappily.)

What is it now?

PIERRE. I couldn't get the rest of it.

MARIE. What rest of it?

PIERRE. That you would actually get up and accept the award. They want me to accept for both of us.

MARIE. I'm supposed to sit in the audience and *watch?* Like an assistant?

PIERRE. I called Dr. Törnebladh. I couldn't budge him.

(MARIE rises, agitated.)

MARIE. *(to the audience)* Is this astonishing? They'll give me the prize, but they won't let me up on the stage to accept it.

(TÖRNEBLADH goes to MARIE downstage.)

(SLIDE: NOBEL HALL)

And of course I have to be gracious to the president of the academy. Törnebladh. So smooth, so effortlessly insulting...oily and slippery, like a raw herring...*(turning suddenly to TÖRNEBLADH)* Dr. Törnebladh! I'm so sorry we couldn't have been here in December.

TÖRNEBLADH. Not at all.

MARIE. I wasn't feeling well. And we had teaching commitments. I was very sorry to miss the official ceremony.

TÖRNEBLADH. His majesty understood. He was very gracious. I do think you would have liked the little talk I gave about you and Pierre.

MARIE. I'm sure I would have.

TÖRNEBLADH. I said your work with Professor Curie was the best illustration of the old proverb, "coninucta valent." Union is strength.

MARIE. *(graciously)* Ah. Very nice.

TÖRNEBLADH. And then I said – you'll enjoy this – "This makes us look at God's word in an entirely new light: 'It is not good that the man should be alone; I will make an helpmeet for him.'"

MARIE. Helpmeet.

TÖRNEBLADH. I was really delighted when I came up with that. I think it handles a delicate situation very well, don't you? Excuse me. I think we're ready for the lecture.

*(**TÖRNEBLADH** holds out a chair for **MARIE** and pats it, pointedly seating her in the audience. She gives the chair a sour look and sits. **TÖRNEBLADH**, his back to us, addresses the Nobel Hall.)*

Distinguished guests, ladies and gentlemen, it is my great honor to present Professor Pierre Curie.

MARIE. *(to the audience)* Is there something wrong with this man?

(Sound: applause)

*(**PIERRE**, at the lectern with his back to us, mimes speaking to the hall.)*

I don't understand, does being a woman require invisibility? The tiniest speck of radium can glow in the dark, but a full-grown woman? No. Please get back in the slag. Your presence is becoming unsettlingly obvious. Please be invisible…I'm sorry, but I exist.

(Sound: Applause.)

*(**PIERRE** hands **MARIE** her Nobel award and, none too happily, they pose for a photograph.)*

(SLIDE: THE FRONT PAGE OF A NEWSPAPER,
showing **MARIE** *and* **PIERRE** *posing solemnly)*

(SLIDE: MARIE AND PIERRE'S LIVING ROOM)

PIERRE. I hate this. I truly hate it.

MARIE. I hate it, too, but we can be civil.

PIERRE. We can't get our work done. What's the point of all this?

MARIE. Well, I hope the point is it will help us fund the work. Maybe we'll get an actual lab.

PIERRE. But, what have these absurd interviews actually produced? Nothing. Well, not nothing – requests for my scintillating presence, for autographs. For loans. *(taking out an envelope)* Here, how about this?...A letter from a total stranger asking if I would mind sending him a thousand francs by return mail. If I had a thousand francs I would buy a pistol and shoot the next journalist who comes through the door.

MARIE. Pierre, please. You're making yourself upset.

PIERRE. The imbecile who asked me about chickens. He was serious.

MARIE. Chickens...

PIERRE. Did I agree with the idea that radium could be used to make chickens lay hard-boiled eggs. You don't think he should have been taken out and shot? *(touching his chest)* A column of bile is rising in my esophagus like mercury in a thermometer.

(Sound: a knock at the door)

MARIE. Please. Try to smile.

*(**MARIE** brings **TERBOUGIE** into the room.)*

Pierre, this is Mr. Terbougie.

PIERRE. Yes. I'm sure it is.

TERBOUGIE. Mr. Curie, it's a great pleasure to see you again. A pleasure and an honor.

PIERRE. I'm sorry, we've met?

TERBOUGIE. Years ago. I doubt if you'd remember. We were on a committee to save Dreyfus. What a travesty that whole affair was. But you were brilliant.

PIERRE. I see.

MARIE. How can we help you with your article, Mr. Terbougie?

(**PIERRE** *looks at his pocket watch.*)

PIERRE. We can give you seven minutes.

TERBOUGIE. Yes, well, I suppose the technical bits are a little beyond most readers, but I wonder if we could talk about the personal side of your discoveries.

PIERRE. The personal side of radiation?

TERBOUGIE. Well, of you and Madame Curie.

PIERRE. We're married.

TERBOUGIE. Yes…

PIERRE. To each other.

TERBOUGIE. Yes.

PIERRE. *(astonished he might want to know more)* I believe that covers it.

TERBOUGIE. Well, of course, it's unusual for a husband and wife to share a love not only for each other, but for science as well. What is that like? Is it the romantic idyll in a scientific lab we've read about?

(*He smiles, sharing the joke.*)

PIERRE. *Romantic idyll?*

MARIE. *(jumping in)* Pierre and I feel that it's the science that matters, not the person.

TERBOUGIE. Yes, of course. But, I remember how eloquent you were during the Dreyfus days. I wonder if you have an anecdote about your work on radium.

PIERRE. An anecdote.

TERBOUGIE. Does anything come to mind?

PIERRE. I'm pleased to tell you my mind is a total and complete blank.

(**PIERRE** *pointedly winds his pocket watch.*)

TERBOUGIE. Well, I don't want to take too much of your time, but...

PIERRE. *(jumping to his feet and shaking* **TERBOUGIE**'s *hand)* Thank you. Can't tell you how much I appreciate that. We have an enormous amount of work to do. Pleasure meeting you. Meeting you again. A real pleasure. Right this way.

*(**PIERRE** leads him to the door.)*

MARIE. I hope you got what you needed.

TERBOUGIE. Yes, I'll be fine. Thank you. Mrs. Curie, it was a pleasure to have...

PIERRE. Don't forget your umbrella.

*(**PIERRE** presses his umbrella to him. **PIERRE** and **TERBOUGIE** freeze in place.)*

MARIE. No, wait. "...Don't forget your umbrella." That was the day. "Don't forget your umbrella."

*(**MARIE** turns back to the living room. **PIERRE** and **TERBOUGIE** return to their places from just before **TERBOUGIE**'s exit.)*

TERBOUGIE. Mrs. Curie, it was a pleasure to have...

PIERRE. Don't forget your umbrella.

*(**TERBOUGIE** is gone.)*

MARIE. Well, I wonder what that interview will look like.

PIERRE. Exactly like the others. They make it all up. Let's pull ourselves together and go to the lab.

MARIE. Now?

PIERRE. We haven't put any time in today on our "romantic idyll".

MARIE. I can't yet. I have to take care of the children first.

PIERRE. What do you have to do?

MARIE. I have to feed them.

PIERRE. Can't someone else do that?

MARIE. Once I go to the lab, I won't see them for the rest of the day. They need a few minutes with me.

PIERRE. *I* need you. I need to work. We've spent the whole morning making ourselves stupid.

MARIE. After I feed the children.

(MARIE heads for another room.)

PIERRE. How long will you be?

MARIE. I don't know.

PIERRE. Are you coming at all?

MARIE. I don't *know.* Don't torment me!

(MARIE exits.)

(Sound: a crack of thunder)

(SLIDE: A PARIS STREET. RAIN FALLING)

(Sound: the roar of an approaching wagon and another clap of thunder)

(With the exception of MARIE, the CAST is onstage, holding open umbrellas.)

ÉMILE. Pierre steps into the Rue Dauphine, near the Pont Neuf, just as a huge wagon, thirty-feet long is coming fast in the other direction. In the driving rain, under his umbrella, Pierre doesn't see it.

(PIERRE is handed an umbrella.)

PIERRE. As he tries to hurry across the street, on legs weakened from years of exposure to radiation. He steps out from behind a carriage, and there, suddenly, the wagon is bearing down on him. As one of the horses brushes him, he grabs the animal's harness, trying not to fall. But the horse shies and Pierre falls to the pavement. The driver pulls the wagon sharply to the side and the front wheels just miss Pierre. People watching from the sidewalk expel a sigh of relief. But the driver can't pull the wagon far enough away from him, and the rear wheel crushes Pierre's skull.

(The moment is punctuated as they close their umbrellas. PIERRE exits. ÉMILE and PAUL enter. They look ashen. MARIE is in a chair.)

(SLIDE: MARIE AND PIERRE'S LIVING ROOM)

MARIE. What is it? What happened?

PAUL. Pierre...

ÉMILE. He was crossing the street. By the Pont Neuf... *(He can't go on.)*

MARIE. What? He's not hurt...?

ÉMILE. There was a huge wagon...

MARIE. How bad is it?

*(**ÉMILE** and **PAUL** find it hard to speak.)*

Pierre is dead? Dead? Absolutely dead?

ÉMILE. Maybe he was holding the umbrella so that he couldn't see the wagon.

PAUL. Or...maybe his legs gave out.

MARIE. Where is he?

ÉMILE. They're bringing him here. You should take the children and wait at my house.

MARIE. No, I'm not leaving. Can the children stay with you for a day or two?

ÉMILE. Yes, of course. But shouldn't you be...?

MARIE. I'm waiting here for Pierre.

*(**PAUL** and **ÉMILE** withdraw.)*

I wait for four hours. When they bring you in, they tell me to leave so they can remove your clothes. I'm stunned and I obey. How could I be so crazy? It was my job to take off your bloody rags. After they leave, I throw the shreds into a huge fire – with clotted blood and the debris of your brain still on them. In the horror of the moment, I kiss what is left of you in all that. Your lips, that I used to call greedy, are pale and discolored. I kiss those eyelids you closed so often so that I could touch them with my lips. Pierre... I had to take care of the children. I told you not to torment me, and those were the last words I spoke to you. But, I had to take care of the children.

(SLIDE: WE SEE SPRING THROUGH MARGUERITE'S WINDOW.)

MARGUERITE. *(writing in her journal)* Finally, spring. Periwinkles and hyacinth! And little blue buds on the rosemary plants. At last, this dismal year has melted away and now – just watch us come alive again.

*(Depressed, **MARIE** slowly covers her lab equipment with a cloth. She goes to her desk and opens her journal.)*

(SLIDE: MARIE'S LAB)

MARIE. Pierre, I woke up this morning a little calmer, but then within a quarter of an hour I was howling like a wild animal. I walk down the street as if hypnotized. I don't really care about anything. I won't kill myself. I don't even have the desire for that. But I think sometimes, why can't a wagon come by and take me the way it took my beloved.

JEANNE. *(entering)* Marie, please, you have to pull yourself out of it. That diary of grief you're keeping just makes it worse. Look at it this way: At least you had someone who loved you all these years. You should realize how lucky you are.

MARIE. Lucky?

JEANNE. That may sound cold, but it's the truth. Some of us drew an unlucky hand.

MARIE. You don't mean Paul. He's devoted to you.

JEANNE. Really? Devoted? This morning, he called me "insolent." Twice. *Insolent.* You don't know how harsh he is with me. And he does nothing to better our lives. He could have taken a position this year with a large company. We could be enjoying our lives instead of squeezing by. You're lucky. You should be grateful.

MARIE. Jeanne, this is not the best time to get into this – but how can you ask Paul to do industrial work? If he were designing dynamos someplace, how could he have done his paper on Brownian motion?

JEANNE. Oh my God, I went to his lecture on that. What was all *that* about?

MARIE. You have no idea how brilliant he is, do you?

JEANNE. Help me to understand this. Seriously. Why can't he work in an industrial lab? He'd still be doing science. And he'd be doing something useful. Not just theory.

MARIE. Maybe he doesn't have a choice. Theory can be intoxicating.

JEANNE. That's what I mean. He's drunk on it. Why does he put his own pleasure ahead of his family?

MARIE. It's not always pleasure. Sometimes it's torture. But, the drive to – I don't know, to see into the dark. It's so powerful it can make you helpless. It's irresistible. Very few people are capable of knowing something that was never known before, by anyone. And Paul is one of them. He's one of the few people alive who is capable of that.

JEANNE. Yes, I know. He's very clever.

MARIE. *(frustrated)* No – Jeanne – brilliant. He explained Brownian motion more simply than Einstein did – in a completely original way. Paul created a whole new kind of mathematics...

JEANNE. Yes, it's very exciting. But it doesn't give him the right to call me insolent. Well, I shouldn't be surprised. I always feel a little bit of contempt from Paul because I'm not smart enough. You don't know how awful I feel sometimes when all you smart ones are talking. What am I supposed to do? All I wanted was to make a home for him – to raise our children. But he'd rather talk shop with strangers than spend a few simple minutes with me. I can't talk about ordinary things with the man, about my day. I can't. I get nervous. My palms sweat. The loneliness is unbearable.

MARIE. I had no idea...

JEANNE. *(looking away)* I can't help it if I'm not brilliant. I try to keep up with all of you, but I can't. Yes, all right, I want him to earn a little more – because all I have to offer is to make him a nice home. But I don't even have that chance to please him. *(wiping her eyes)* I'm telling you – you're lucky. You've had a good life, Marie, but you have a talent for suffering.

MARIE. A talent for suffering?

JEANNE. You excel at it. Listen, life is too precious. Stop burying yourself in grief. Put a smile on your face. You might start to believe it.

(SLIDE: MARIE'S NEW LAB)

MARIE. I came to the lab. This beautiful new place you never got to see. I tried to make measurements and add points to a curve the way you and I have done so many times. I tried, but I couldn't.

(PAUL enters. He wears a hat.)

PAUL. *(smiling)* This is wonderful, you can breathe in here!

MARIE. It's better than the old lab, anyway.

PAUL. What will you miss most about that place? The coal dust in your experiments? The rain coming through the ceiling?

MARIE. What will I miss most?

PAUL. *(gently)* I know. Of course. That's not a very good start, is it? Anyway. I didn't come to see the lab.

MARIE. No?

PAUL. Are you working? Actually working?

MARIE. Not very much.

PAUL. You have to. You can't just stop.

MARIE. Yes, well, it's kind of difficult. I get the beginning of an idea and I look across the room to tell him, the way I have a thousand times before. And I'm looking into empty space.

PAUL. You know, you said the one thing you couldn't do was let someone else isolate radium. I heard you say it.

MARIE. I'm trying to work. It's difficult.

PAUL. Look, There's almost certainly a prize in it for who-ever gets it down to a pure metal. Radium is yours. If you stop now, it's going to be someone else's.

MARIE. *(firmly)* I know. I'm trying.

PAUL. Right. *(Trying another tack)* What about *Kelvin?*

MARIE. What about him?

PAUL. ...Saying you don't really have a new element, that it's just a compound of *other* elements.

MARIE. Kelvin didn't think Röntgen had x-rays, either. Kelvin's a little slow to catch on.

PAUL. But, he'll keep on saying that until he sees pure radium metal, sitting there at the bottom of a dish – won't he? ...Won't he?

MARIE. *(avoiding the discussion)* You haven't really seen the place. *(pointing across the room)* I'm keeping this corner of the room for when the children come in on Thursdays for chemistry.

PAUL. Good. What did Mouton say? Did you ask him?

MARIE. He said yes. He'll teach the natural sciences at his house. Perrin will do basic concepts in phys-ics. Henriette will do history. And you're doing Mathematics. No?

PAUL. Yes, of course. Yes.

MARIE. You sound a little tentative.

PAUL. I'm still talking it over with Jeanne. I'll work it out.

MARIE. Why? What is it?

PAUL. We have a room that would be perfect for a class-room – the children would love it. She absolutely refuses. She's being incredibly prickly about this.

MARIE. Paul, please don't take this the wrong way. Is it pos-sible you're too...I don't know...too hard on her?

PAUL. Are you serious?

MARIE. I know it's none of my business.

PAUL. Do you have any idea how she behaves when our friends aren't around? And her mother is worse. When the two of them get together it's not safe to be in the house.

MARIE. Maybe if you were gentler with her…

PAUL. Marie, do you understand what I'm telling you?

MARIE. Just a kind word once in a while…

PAUL. *(overlapping)* I'm telling you, it's not safe. You want to see what she's like? You want to actually see it?

MARIE. *(overlapping)* She can't be so bad you can't give her a kind word once in a while.

PAUL. All right, look.

(**PAUL** *takes off his hat. There's a bandage on his head.*)

MARIE. What happened to your head?

PAUL. She broke a bottle over it.

MARIE. My God, she could have killed you.

PAUL. Last week, she and her mother took turns throwing iron chairs at me. One after the other. Iron chairs.

MARIE. Why?

PAUL. Well, predominantly, because they're insane. They're obsessed with money. I can't leave cash in the house or they steal it. I hid some in the chandelier and they found it.

MARIE. In the chandelier?

PAUL. It would be funny except that my life is hell. I had no idea I was marrying a lunatic. I'm paying for youthful inexperience, not for any lack of gentleness. If it weren't for my children, I would have left her years ago.

MARIE. I'm so sorry. Sit down. Let me see your head.

PAUL. It's fine.

MARIE. Sit. Did you wash the wound?

(**PAUL** *sits.*)

PAUL. It was running like a faucet.

MARIE. Be still. Let me look at it.

(**MARIE** *tends to his head with alcohol.*)

PAUL. The woman is a dangerous lunatic.

MARIE. Hold still. Does this hurt?

PAUL. *(wincing)* No…*(beat)* Thank you. Marie, you can't stop working.

MARIE. Paul…

PAUL. You have to follow your mind – wherever it goes.

MARIE. I'm *trying*. But, doing the most ordinary things without him is like a betrayal. I feel like I'm changing.

PAUL. You're supposed to. Everything changes. Even the elements can change.

MARIE. Mnn. The unstable ones.

PAUL. You think it's a weakness to change? It's not, it's strength. It's nature. How can you not see that? You're going through exactly what you described: "Violent interior movement in a substance that radiates energy," and over time the substance changes: uranium into Thorium, thorium into radium. Someone as radiant as you couldn't exist without transforming. Transmutation is your absolute destiny!

MARIE. You're not trying to be funny, are you?

PAUL. I'm completely serious.

MARIE. Well, it *is* funny, what you just said.

PAUL. You're not laughing. You're not even smiling.

MARIE. I haven't smiled in several years. But, what about you?

PAUL. What?

MARIE. Change. How long will you be in a situation where people throw chairs at you and hit you with bottles? How can you tolerate it?

PAUL. I'm in the thrall of diamagnetism.

MARIE. Diamagnetism.

PAUL. You put a highly magnetic object like my psychotic wife next to an ordinarily non-magnetic object, like me, and if conditions are right, then, eventually, there will be repulsion. That's what's happening to me. I am being transformed. When the process is complete, I'll be propelled from her with an astonishing force.

MARIE. I see. But – now forgive me – this is your area. I wouldn't presume to tell you about magnetism…

PAUL. No, go on…

MARIE. What about paramagnetism? Not diamagnetism, but paramagnetism.

PAUL. What about it?

MARIE. Can't the opposite happen? Doesn't a highly magnetic source sometimes transform an object into one that's attractive? Can't you experience an attraction that never lets you escape? Will you start to look forward to your chair and bottle every night?

PAUL. No. Because the paramagnetic is entirely dependent on temperature, and that's a susceptibility that is…

MARIE. …That's inversely proportional to temperature, and…

PAUL. …Exactly. And the temperature in my house is far too high for those attractive forces ever to take over.

MARIE. Because every atom has a permanent magnetic moment…right?

PAUL. Yes, that's…

MARIE. …And when there is no magnetic field, the atomic moments all point randomly…

PAUL. …Because of thermal effects…

MARIE. But, in the presence of a field, the moments align along the field direction. And that's when the attraction occurs.

PAUL. Yes.

MARIE. Yes. Right. I love that.

(*The tension between them has grown. Their faces are close. They lean in and kiss. After a moment, they kiss again.* PAUL *rises to leave, but pauses at the door for one last look at* MARIE. *He freezes in the doorway, as…*)

(*Light change: down on* PAUL *and up on* PIERRE *as he lights his pipe.*)

MARIE. (*turning to* PIERRE) You know you're irreplaceable. You do know that…?

(PIERRE *shrugs.*)

I wish I knew if you could hear any of this – when I talk.

PIERRE. I very much doubt it, don't you?

MARIE. Well, then why did you keep dragging me to Eusapia Palladino's place for all those séances?

PIERRE. Because I couldn't figure out how she moved the damned table.

MARIE. No one could ever replace you. I wish you could know that.

PIERRE. One night in the shed I was hobbling around on sore legs. And all of a sudden you were anxious – about the future. You were like a little girl, asking for reassurance. "If one of us were to die …"

MARIE. If one of us were to die before the other…what would we do?

PIERRE. We would go on working. Things go on.

MARIE. But, with someone else…?

PIERRE. *(shrugging)* It *all* goes on. Doesn't it?

(**PIERRE** *exits.*)

(*Light change. Lights up on* **PAUL** *in the doorway.*)

PAUL. Please, Marie. Start with a *little* work. Just a little. Where's your obsession when you need it?

MARIE. *(smiling)* I'll try. I will.

PAUL. There. You smiled.

(**PAUL** *exits.*)

(*SLIDE: ÉMILE'S STUDY AT HOME*)

MARGUERITE. I don't like what's going on in the lab.

ÉMILE. Neither do I. She's getting weaker. She has no color anymore. Her fingers are cracking open again. It's like what happened to Pierre's legs.

MARGUERITE. What are you talking about?

ÉMILE. The radium.

MARGUERITE. I'm talking about Paul. He goes to the lab and confides in her. They commiserate with each other about losing Pierre. She's vulnerable now. And he looks at her with those eyes of his and confides in her.

ÉMILE. What are we supposed to do?

MARGUERITE. Can't you take him aside and hint at what this could lead to? Just a little hint?

ÉMILE. I hate hinting. I don't like giving hints and I don't like getting them. Why can't people say what they mean? You're not hinting now, are you?

MARGUERITE. At what?

ÉMILE. That this is somehow my fault?

MARGUERITE. No, but can't you say something? Can't you gently remind him of what they could be getting themselves into?

ÉMILE. Well, it happens I actually have said something. Pointedly.

MARGUERITE. You have.

ÉMILE. Yes.

MARGUERITE. What did you say?

ÉMILE. We were standing by the fig tree in Marie's garden, and I said, "Tell me, how's Jeanne doing?"

MARGUERITE. That's it?

ÉMILE. *(erupting a little)* You see? You see how totally ineffective hinting is? I put the subject of his wife squarely on the table and he just ignored It. He said, "Oh, she's all right." And then he lowered his voice and he said, "You know how it is."

MARGUERITE. He said, "You know how it is?" That was a perfect opening.

ÉMILE. How do you get an opening out of that?

MARGUERITE. If a woman said that to me, it would be the beginning of an intense conversation.

ÉMILE. I wouldn't be surprised.

MARGUERITE. We can't just let her get in bed with a married man! We have an obligation.

ÉMILE. Not me. My obligation stops at the edge of the duvet!

(SLIDE: MARIE'S GARDEN)

*(ÉMILE, MARGUERITE, JEANNE and PAUL gather in
the garden.)*

PAUL. *(to ÉMILE)* You have to realize – they're going to put
up an enormous fight.

ÉMILE. Why would the Academy turn her down? Can she
hear us?

MARGUERITE. She's still upstairs, getting dressed. *(an
encouraging sign:)* I think she was at the lab all day.

PAUL. Good! *(to ÉMILE)* Seriously, we have to be prepared
for a fight.

ÉMILE. Why? Who have they got besides Marie?

PAUL. Edward Branly.

ÉMILE. Branly! Please. He doesn't come near Marie.

PAUL. But he's Catholic. That's very fashionable now.

ÉMILE. Well, she's Polish. Isn't she Catholic, too?

PAUL. Branly is *professionally* Catholic.

ÉMILE. No, this is ridiculous. She's the only Nobel Prize
winner in France who's *not* in the Academy…why
would they turn her down?

JEANNE. Well, for God's sake, isn't it obvious? Because she's
a woman.

ÉMILE. There's nothing in the by-laws that explicitly pre-
vents it. We've checked.

JEANNE. There never has been a female member of the
French Academy and there never will be.

MARGUERITE. I don't believe that for a minute.

JEANNE. Oh, face facts. I'm all for women doing as they
please, but we have to be realistic.

PAUL. What about Becquerel? Would he help?

ÉMILE. He would *say* he was helping. The first time they
nominated Pierre it was Becquerel who sank him. We
should ask his advice, then do the opposite.

JEANNE. I can't understand all this politicking. Isn't science
a search for the truth?

PAUL. Jeanne, it's a little more complicated than that.

MARGUERITE. Oh my God, look…

JEANNE. What…?

(MARIE enters from offstage. She is wearing a white dress with a red rose at her waist. Her face is serene and undistracted. She carries a tray of bread and cheese.)

MARIE. I got the most delicious chèvre from a farmer just outside the village. You have to try this.

(They're mystified by this sudden change.)

Irene can't understand why I love chèvre so much. She says to her little sister, "You know our mother is very smart, but she doesn't know that goat cheese smells like goats." *(chuckling good-naturedly)* I'll get some more wine.

(MARIE exits the stage.)

ÉMILE. Who was *that*?

MARGUERITE. Maybe she found a new element.

JEANNE. *(darkly)* You think so?

PAUL. *(tasting the cheese, as if nothing has happened.)* Mmm. It *is* good.

(He holds out the plate to JEANNE, who just skewers him with a long, piercing look. ÉMILE hums a few bars of Beethoven's Ode to Joy. MARGUERITE stops him with a poke in the arm.)

(SLIDE: PAUL AND JEANNE'S BEDROOM)

(JEANNE takes a gulp of cognac and, slightly tipsy, slams her glass down on a table.)

PAUL. Would you please stop drinking?

JEANNE. I don't think you have the right to ask me to stop anything, do you?

PAUL. What have I done? What? I've done nothing to hurt you.

JEANNE. I'm not stupid. "Oh, let's take the sewing room and use it to school the children." Just so you can serve her insane ideas. You're a professor of physics, and you're going to teach arithmetic to nine year-olds? You're willing to humiliate yourself for her.

PAUL. She has a perfectly reasonable idea.

JEANNE. Which is what?

PAUL. To give all our children the benefit of the best minds and get them off on the right foot. Émile is totally committed to it.

JEANNE. Émile is a fool.

PAUL. Please. Don't trot out your ignorance. He's one of the greatest mathematicians in France.

JEANNE. Yes? What about his "infinite monkey theorem?"

PAUL. What about it?

JEANNE. A monkey hitting the keys of a typewriter for an infinite amount of time will almost surely produce the works of *Shakespeare?* Come *on.*

PAUL. Don't disparage what you don't understand. He's talking about probabilities. The probability of something like that is miniscule, but not zero.

JEANNE. Yes, I'm sure it is. What do you do on the train?

PAUL. What?

JEANNE. You ride the train with her every day to Paris. What goes on during those trips?

PAUL. Sometimes we work. Sometimes we talk about physics.

JEANNE. How intellectual. Have you come up with a formula yet to get your hand up her dress?

PAUL. How dare you say that.

JEANNE. Why not? I don't think the probability of that is zero, do you?

PAUL. Shut your mouth. Shut it. You can't talk that way to me.

JEANNE. Oh, right. It's not her body. It's her *mind* you love. You're being seduced by an egomaniacal woman with a pipe dream. If she ever sees anything in the bottom of a dish, it will be her own reflection.

PAUL. You don't even know how ignorant you are of science.

JEANNE. Fine. Let's be scientific. I know what I know, but let's say I'm wrong. I could be wrong – I'm only human. If I'm right, though, if you give me the slightest proof that I'm right, then…and this is only rational…I'll have to take a reasonable, deliberate action.

PAUL. Which is what?

JEANNE. Well, I suppose I'll have to kill one of you.

(Smiling, she takes her cognac into the other room.)

END ACT ONE

ACT TWO

ÉMILE. *(to audience)* If you leave your classroom and head south on the Boulevard Saint Jacques, turn left on Port Royal, right on Avenue Gobelins and left on Rue du Banquier, you'll be there. Number 5, Rue Banquier is only a short, pleasant walk from the Sorbonne. Up on the fifth floor is a modest two-room apartment where a professor can rest between classes. Put his feet up, read a book.

(SLIDE: THE APARTMENT ON RUE BANQUIER)

*(**PAUL** is stretched out on the bed, reading. **MARIE**, in her customary dark dress, enters. She drops her briefcase and gives **PAUL** a long kiss. She sits on the bed and starts undoing her shoes.)*

MARIE. We don't have much time.

PAUL. How long do you have?

MARIE. An hour and thirteen minutes.

PAUL. That's all?

MARIE. It would have been less. I ran most of the way.

PAUL. You shouldn't run. You should rest as much as you can.

(He kisses her fingers.)

MARIE. Don't act like I'm dying. It's very unromantic.

PAUL. You didn't faint in your living room…

MARIE. I did, but it was just a little.

PAUL. …Your daughter didn't walk in and find you on the floor…

MARIE. I explained it to her. She's fine.

PAUL. Can't you slow down?

43

MARIE. And let someone else get there before me... that would be nice, wouldn't it?

(**PAUL** *holds her hand.*)

PAUL. Look what's happened to your fingers. You have dizzy spells, you faint...

MARIE. Please. I get a little tired. Sometimes I pass out. That's hardly dying. I'm actually pretty strong.

(*She pulls him down on the bed and gives him a long kiss. Finally he has to come up for air.*)

PAUL. That's impressive. How did you get so strong?

MARIE. Stirring ten tons of slag. You should try it.

PAUL. I don't think so. Stirring is women's work.

(**MARIE** *grabs his nose and pinches.*)

MARIE. Say you're sorry for that.

PAUL. Let go. That hurts.

MARIE. Say you're sorry.

PAUL. I'm sorry.

MARIE. What were you doing at 10:23 today? Exactly 10:23.

PAUL. I don't know. What were you doing?

MARIE. Thinking about your eyes. God. They're beautiful. I was telling my students about the half-life of polonium and all I could see were your eyes.

(**MARIE** *gently kisses his eyes.* **PIERRE** *lights his pipe. This memory of* **PIERRE** *is too powerful for* **MARIE**. *She looks away.*)

PAUL. What is it?

MARIE. Nothing. I'm all right.

PAUL. (*confused*) What's the matter?

MARIE. I can't lose you.

PAUL. You won't.

MARIE. I couldn't bear it if I lost you.

PAUL. Why would you lose me?

MARIE. Do you still sleep with her? You do, don't you?

PAUL. We're married. Yes.

MARIE. You sleep in the same bed, and you make love.

PAUL. Sometimes, yes.

MARIE. You can't do that.

PAUL. Are you serious?

MARIE. I don't trust her. Listen to me. If she can, she'll get pregnant. If she presents you with another baby, she'll tie you to her completely. You'll never get away.

PAUL. She won't do that.

MARIE. She knows how principled you are and she plays on that. What if there were a beautiful little baby lying there? How could you walk out on that?

PAUL. How can I suddenly announce I'm not sleeping with her anymore?

MARIE. Tell her you have to stay up late to prepare your lectures. You have to leave early in the morning. You don't want to disturb her, so you sleep in another room. I don't know – tell her something. I can't bear the thought of you being with her. It tears my heart out.

PAUL. You're not going to lose me. I couldn't survive without you.

MARIE. *(lightly, teasing)* You used to bring me a flower when you came here. I haven't seen one of those in a while.

PAUL. Tomorrow you'll have a bouquet.

MARIE. And you managed not to answer my letter.

PAUL. What letter?

MARIE. When you and she went to Brittany.

PAUL. *(puzzled)* What letter?

MARIE. I sent you a letter…oh my God. What if she saw it? What if she found it and read it?

PAUL. I never got a letter from you in Brittany.

(**MARIE** *goes the table and opens the drawer. She takes out the letters and goes through them.*)

MARIE. Is it in with these?

PAUL. Marie, I never saw it.

(**MARIE** *puts the letters back in the drawer and starts throwing on her coat.*)

Where are you going?

MARIE. Émile said he was dropping off a paper at your house today.

PAUL. I know. What are you...

MARIE. I have to talk to him before he sees her.

PAUL. Be careful what you say. What are you going to tell him?

MARIE. I don't know – she might have come across an innocent, collegial letter. She might have misunderstood. Something like that.

PAUL. Are you coming back?

MARIE. Yes! Don't move.

(SLIDE: ÉMILE'S OFFICE)

(**ÉMILE** *is at the blackboard, writing equations.* **MARIE** *enters, breathless.*)

MARIE. You haven't taken your paper to Paul's house yet, have you?

ÉMILE. I got caught up in this.

MARIE. Could I ask you a favor when you go there? I have this strange feeling that I might have offended Jeanne in some way. She's been a little odd with me lately. ... You think it's possible that...? That...no. I doubt it.

ÉMILE. What?

MARIE. No, it's silly. I really doubt it.

ÉMILE. What is it?

MARIE. I sent Paul a letter while they were in Brittany. It was an innocent letter about his work. But it was written in... I don't know – in a friendly way. Collegial. If she saw it somehow, you think she might have misunderstood?

ÉMILE. She misunderstands whatever she can.

MARIE. I wonder if she's opening his mail. She can be jealous.

ÉMILE. Oh my God. We were on the metro once and Paul gave up his seat to a young woman, and Jeanne harangued him from Porte Maillot all the way to Vincennes.

MARIE. She might be looking for things to...you know, to get excited about.

ÉMILE. I wouldn't be surprised.

MARIE. Even though it was entirely innocent.

ÉMILE. Yes. Of course. I'll see if she mentions a letter.

MARIE. I wouldn't bring it up if she doesn't...

ÉMILE. *(overlapping)* No...

MARIE. *(overlapping)* There's no sense in...

ÉMILE. *(overlapping)* ...No sense making her crazier than she already is.

(*SLIDE: THE LANGEVIN HOUSE*)

(**JEANNE** *slams the letter down on the table.*)

JEANNE. She'll go straight to hell! God in Heaven will send this woman to Hell. Her eyeballs will melt and run down her cheeks. Do I have the proof? Is this the proof, or isn't it?

ÉMILE. Jeanne, they're colleagues. I'm sure it's completely inno...

JEANNE. No! No! I have the proof. "With all my heart, M." That's how she signs it. That's innocent? No, professor, don't delude yourself. Colleagues don't have hearts. She's stealing my husband! This wretched woman is stealing my life!!

ÉMILE. Is it possible that...?

JEANNE. No! It's not possible. Why is he treating me like this? Isn't it humiliating enough, the way he goes on with all of you in front of me, when he knows I don't understand, with that little smirk at my ignorance – isn't it enough that I come home from these dinner parties and cry myself to sleep? I hold in my sobs so he won't hear me!

ÉMILE. Jeanne, there's nothing in the letter but the word "heart." Maybe you should have a good long talk with Paul...

JEANNE. Oh, we'll have a talk. When they all gather around to say what a great woman she was. What a great humanitarian. We'll have a nice, long talk. Maybe then he'll understand what he's forcing me to do.

ÉMILE. I'm sorry...I don't under...

JEANNE. It's simple, professor. I have an obstacle in my path. The obstacle will be removed. That's clear, isn't it? Isn't that perfectly clear?

ÉMILE. Well, no.

JEANNE. Don't over-intellectualize it. The obstacle. Yes?

ÉMILE. Yes...?

JEANNE. ...Will be removed.

ÉMILE. Oh.

JEANNE. Émile, I'm surprised you don't have a musical interlude for that.

(SLIDE. MARIE'S LAB)

(MARIE is stirring a steaming pot. PAUL is watching, a bit agitated.)

MARIE. I don't understand, What does she mean, "obstacle?" What's the obstacle?

PAUL. *You.* She's threatening to kill you.

MARIE. *(stopping her stirring)* No.

PAUL. Of course she is. She may be capable of it, too.

(After a beat of stunned silence, MARIE takes the pot off the fire.)

Can I help you with that?

MARIE. I'm fine.

(MARIE sits at her apparatus.)

(carefully placing a sample on the balance) It's completely irrational, what she said. She must be in terrible pain.

PAUL. She makes sure *other* people are in pain. When she can't get what she wants she goes completely crazy.

MARIE. *(putting down the sample)* God, I can't concentrate. I can't *think.*

(**PAUL** *puts a hand on her shoulder and gently massages it.*)

PAUL. Why don't you take a break?

MARIE. *(considering it, she indicates the pot)* That solution has to sit for a while and crystallize.

PAUL. How long do we have?

MARIE. Approximately two hours.

PAUL. *(smiling)* Approximately?

MARIE. …And ten minutes.

PAUL. We can't go there together. You go first. I'll come up in a few minutes.

(**MARIE** *starts to go, but turns to him.*)

MARIE. Don't you hate this? Sneaking around like this?

PAUL. What choice do we have?

MARIE. What *choice* do we have.

(**MARIE** *lets these words sink in on both of them. She exits.*)

(SLIDE: THE APARTMENT ON RUE BANQUIER)

(**MARIE** *is pacing as* **PAUL** *enters.*)

PAUL. Did anyone see you come in?

MARIE. I *hate* this. I hate sneaking into the building like this. And I hate betraying Jeanne. I can't stand it. We should just come out with it.

PAUL. Come out with it? What do you mean?

MARIE. I want to live with you. Don't you want us to live together?

PAUL. Yes, but how?

MARIE. How? By ending your marriage.

PAUL. I don't think you know her. She would make sure I never saw my children again. Jeanne would love that. She knows exactly what kind of hell she can put me through.

MARIE. Paul, you're not thinking of leaving me...?

PAUL. How could I leave you?

MARIE. People do things like that. They take the easy way out. It would save you a lot of trouble if you left me.

PAUL. You know how much it hurts to hear you say that?

MARIE. I think you're considering it. Right now. You're running down a list of options, and that's one of them, isn't?

PAUL. It is not an option.

MARIE. Of course it is. We both know it is. The fact that you deny it's an option means you're considering it.

PAUL. I will not leave you.

MARIE. You've said those words to her, too, haven't you? You don't you know what this means to me.

PAUL. Marie. Please. Let's not jump ten moves ahead. She saw a friendly, warm letter. That's all. Not a love letter. We can't let it go beyond that. The first thing we do is burn the letters in that drawer. I hate to do it, but we have to.

(**MARIE** *crosses to the table. She picks up a jar of hand cream.*)

MARIE. Did you put this here?

PAUL. What is it?

MARIE. Hand cream. For my fingers. I always keep it in the bathroom.

(**MARIE** *opens the drawer. Seeing the drawer is empty, she looks up at* **PAUL,** *stunned.*)

(*SLIDE: THE LANGEVIN HOUSE*)

(**JEANNE** *enters with the letters. She ties them with a red ribbon and locks them in a drawer.*)

JEANNE. It's so charming to know that while you were having interminable meals with your wife in Brittany you were longing to smell another woman's hair in Paris.

PAUL. Don't subject me to this, please.

JEANNE. You have a peculiar fascination with her body odor, don't you? Do you suppose you're just a little perverted?

PAUL. How did you get those letters?

JEANNE. Astonishing how you smart people think everyone else is stupid. You parade around with the key to your love nest in your pants pocket, as if no one is clever enough to find it.

PAUL. So you went through my pockets.

JEANNE. Yes. Maybe you should call the police.

PAUL. What did you do, go there in the middle of the night?

JEANNE. Can you imagine how disgusting it was to see her intimate toilet articles arranged on a shelf? And to look at that unmade bed? I suppose intellectuals are above laundering their bedclothes.

PAUL. Jeanne…

JEANNE. Or does the smell of soiled sheets give you an extra thrill?

PAUL. Please…

JEANNE. This thing with her is finished. And if you have any hesitation about ending it this minute, just keep in mind that if I make these letters public, she'll be ruined.

PAUL. Why in the name of God would you make them *public*?

JEANNE. *Why?* What world are you living in? You've humiliated me with a professional woman. It's not as if she were a shop girl. You could be excused for using someone of that class as a receptacle for your male vanity and excess fluids. But a woman who's my equal? No.

That's a deliberate slap in the face. No decent person would accept that. Your little Marie would be an outcast. Her career would be ruined. She's so mentally unstable she would probably kill herself. Which would solve a number of problems.

PAUL. You won't do it. You won't make those letters public.

JEANNE. Really? Why do you suppose not?

PAUL. Because it would ruin me, too. You like money too much to see me ruined.

JEANNE. As if I get anything in the way of money from you. Anyway, I'd be happy to live in an attic as long as I knew you were suffering.

PAUL. Listen to yourself. You hate me. Why don't you just divorce me?

JEANNE. Darling...because I hate you. You will stop seeing this woman. And you'll do it with a letter. There will be no clinging to you, no staining your clothes with tears. No contact. Ever again. Ever.

(SLIDE: THE APARTMENT ON RUE BANQUIER)

(PAUL sits on the bed, waiting, as MARIE enters quickly.)

MARIE. Becquerel walked in just as I was leaving. He was obsessed with chatting.

(MARIE crosses to PAUL and kisses him. She takes off her coat.)

I couldn't get rid of him. He keeps thanking me for citing his work in my papers. Of course I cite his work. I'm scrupulous about that. What he's really doing is reminding me how grand he is. I have to listen to him puffing himself up with exquisite indirection, and all the while I'm thinking of you, waiting for me.

PAUL. Please come over here.

MARIE. I can't just throw my clothes in a pile in the corner.

PAUL. *(smiling)* I adore you.

MARIE. I adore you, too. Now wait, I want to read you something.

(MARIE opens her briefcase and takes out a letter.)

You wrote this a month ago. I carry it with me. She never saw it. *(sitting next to PAUL, reading)* "My Darling. I'm at our place. I wait like a child for the sound of the rustle of your dress as you come up the stairs…" *(kissing him playfully)* "…But I don't think you'll come today because of your beautiful obsession. I think of you at your apparatus, with your furrowed brow and I fall in love with you all over again. I know that someday you'll isolate the pure element and I'm happy to give up this hour to you. I kiss your fingers. Come to me soon." *(looking up from the letter)* I didn't tell Becquerel. I wanted you to be the first one to hear. I did it.

PAUL. You did what?

MARIE. I saw it shining in the bottom of the dish. Pure radium metal.

PAUL. No…

MARIE. Yes! Yesterday afternoon at four o'clock. I did it! I did it!

PAUL. I knew you would. I didn't know when, but I knew you would do it.

MARIE. *(gently, touching his face)* Let's celebrate.

(As she sits, MARIE sees a newspaper on the bed.)

What's this?

PAUL. She gave an interview to Terbougie. He's incredibly sympathetic to her.

MARIE. He's taking her side? He came to our house – I did everything I could to be civil with him. *(reading)* "Once inside the home of Paul Langevin, we were in the presence of a poor mother almost helpless with grief." Well, at least he's objective.

(SLIDE: THE LANGEVIN HOUSE [SPLIT SCREEN WITH THE APARTMENT ON RUE BANQUIER])

JEANNE. If I didn't hope I could win him back, I would never have spoken in public. I hate the thought of

publicity. I love my husband and I would never do anything to jeopardize his career. *(in tears)* But he took
our boys and left me. What could I do?

MARIE. Why did you take the boys away?

PAUL. I wasn't thinking. I was furious. We had said I would
take them on vacation next month. I took them a little
early. She's exaggerating.

JEANNE. He took them to another country and as far as I
know Mrs. Curie went with them.

MARIE. What is she talking about? I went to the Solvay con-
ference.

JEANNE. You know, I have absolute proof of his betrayal.
And even that – even that I would have endured – but
not this. I can't let my children be just…ripped from
my heart.

TERBOUGIE. You say you have proof…

JEANNE. There are letters.

TERBOUGIE. Do you think I might be able to see one?

JEANNE. Oh, no. I don't think so. No, absolutely not. I
don't know why I even mentioned them.

MARIE. They're perfect together. She has fantasies and he
prints them.

PAUL. She has more than fantasies, she has the letters.

MARIE. She wouldn't go *that* far… Would she? She couldn't.
(but knowing she would go that far:) God, we have to do
something. What can we do?

(There is a moment of concern between them. **PAUL** *rises
and exits.)*

(SLIDE: TERBOUGIE'S NEWSPAPER OFFICE)

*(***PAUL*** *enters and confronts* **TERBOUGIE**.*)*

TERBOUGIE. Mr. Langevin. What an honor.

PAUL. Mr. Terbougie, I think you realize that you are threatening the reputation of the most honored woman in
France.

TERBOUGIE. *Am* I?

PAUL. I'm asking you to behave like a gentleman and retract the insinuations you've made about her.

TERBOUGIE. *Are* you.

PAUL. Yes, in fact, I'm demanding it.

TERBOUGIE. Well, for a scientist, that's awfully mannish of you. Would you like a cup of tea? Your heart must be beating like a rabbit's.

PAUL. I'm warning you. Mrs. Curie can claim defamation.

TERBOUGIE. I see. Let me bring you up to date on a little recent history. God turned his back on us and France lost a disastrous war with Prussia precisely because of the kind of extreme secularism and cultish scientism represented by you and Mrs. Curie.

PAUL. You're not serious. The Prussian war was forty years ago.

TERBOUGIE. And we're still paying the price, aren't we? We cannot turn our backs on God without God turning his back on us.

PAUL. What's God got to do with this? You're talking gibberish.

TERBOUGIE. I'm sorry. Let me make it simple for you. We are in a titanic struggle right now, which is very neatly symbolized by two dueling monuments on opposite sides of Paris – the Basillica of Sacré-Cœur up on Monmartre on one side… *(draining his tea cup and placing it upside down on the table)* …and on the other side of the city, the Eiffel Tower. *(reaching into his desk and taking out some letters tied with a red ribbon)* They both rise to the skies – however, one humbly presents its breast to God's mercy, while the other stabs at heaven like a lethal spear. You might say it *thrusts* itself.

(PAUL is transfixed by the letters. He sees they are his and MARIE's.)

PAUL. What is this? What are you…

TERBOUGIE. The construction of Sacré-Cœur has been an act of penance. I only hope God will forgive us for the Eiffel Tower.

(**TERBOUGIE** *puts the letters in his pocket.*)

PAUL. You cynical hypocrite. I won't let you destroy her.

TERBOUGIE. I believe in God, the creator of all things, Mr. Langevin. You believe in your moist little brain. We'll see which one is stronger.

(**PAUL** *turns and leaves.*)

(SLIDE: THE APARTMENT ON RUE BANQUIER)

(**PAUL** *enters and sees a newspaper on the bed.*)

PAUL. Did you read it?

MARIE. Not yet.

PAUL. Don't.

MARIE. Why not?

PAUL. She's like a wild animal, but I never thought she'd do something like *this*. She's brought formal charges against me. The police have the letters.

MARIE. The police!

PAUL. She's filed a criminal charge.

MARIE. What?!

(**MARIE** *picks up the newspaper.*)

PAUL. Marie, please don't read it…

MARIE. "Consorting with a concubine in the marital dwelling…" Concubine.

PAUL. Apparently it's a crime.

MARIE. First of all, I'm not a concubine. And secondly, we never consorted in a marital dwelling.

PAUL. By the time that's established our lives will be destroyed. I'm sure the letters will be presented in evidence…and you'll have to give testimony. Please, put the paper down.

(SLIDE: TERBOUGIE'S NEWSPAPER OFFICE [SPLIT SCREEN WITH THE APARTMENT ON RUE BANQUIER])

TERBOUGIE. This woman is not of our race. She is Polish and probably Jewish. These intellectuals are almost all old acquaintances from the Dreyfus Affair. They live according to a Dreyfusard set of morals and a licentious Ibsenism.

MARIE. What is this? He was on a committee with Pierre to *save* Dreyfus!

TERBOUGIE. It is no wonder she was turned down by the Academy, and that she will be turned out now by the French nation.

PAUL. Marie, don't read anymore. Put it down.

TERBOUGIE. These pedantic half-breeds who fill the German-Jewish Sorbonne will only tarnish themselves, but not the glory of France.

MARIE. My God...

TERBOUGIE. Listen, my dear Professoress – you won't be able to hide this man in your skirts forever. He is nothing but a boor and a coward.

PAUL. Goddamn it. Give me that paper!

(**PAUL**, *angered beyond words, takes the newspaper out of her hands, balls it up and throws it away.*)

(*SLIDE: LECTURE HALL BLACKBOARD. We see a chart of two curves.*)

(**MARIE** *is finishing a lecture to* **STUDENTS** *[played by the other actors].*)

MARIE. ...So, Curve One is the total radiation plotted over time. Curve Two tracks the penetrating rays through 3 centimeters of air and a thin sheet of aluminum. I'll answer questions now. Yes?

STUDENT ONE. Is it true?

MARIE. (*warily*) Is what true?

STUDENT ONE. There was an article in the newspaper...

MARIE. (*guardedly*) About what?

STUDENT ONE. (*slightly embarrassed*) I'm sorry...I mean about the Nobel Prize. Is it true you're getting a *second* Nobel Prize?

MARIE. *(somewhat relieved, but wanting to talk science instead)* Apparently. Yes.

STUDENT TWO. A *second* one?

MARIE. *(a little acerbic)* Yes, one and one makes two.

STUDENT TWO. May we offer our congratulations?

(Applause. A dour look from MARIE.)

MARIE. Does anyone, perhaps, have a question about the radiation curves of radium?

(Hands go up.)

STUDENT ONE. Do you feel it's all been worth it?

MARIE. *Worth* it?

STUDENT ONE. *(retreating from asking about the scandal)* I mean all the hard work and everything. Because after all, radium can be used to cure cancer.

MARIE. *(with mounting passion)* All right, let me explain something. The discovery of radium was not an effort to find something useful. It was done for itself, for the beauty of pure science. Each point on these curves was plotted laboriously, for hours, sometimes days. But there is *beauty* in plotting those points. Outsiders look for miracles in our work, or else they look into our lives for entertaining stories, but they miss totally the exquisite beauty of the points along the curve. *That's* what makes it worth it. Does that answer the question you were – or possibly weren't – asking? Good afternoon.

(SLIDE: SACRÉ-CŒUR AT NIGHT)

(MARIE crosses the stage, walking in Paris at night. She looks up at the cathedral for a moment, then turns upstage.)

(SLIDE: THE STREET OUTSIDE MARIE'S HOUSE)

(JEANNE confronts MARIE, startling her.)

JEANNE. So. You're still seeing him. You want to test how far I'll go? Is that what you want?

MARIE. Please, we should not discus this in the street…

JEANNE. You stand there and listen to me. Read the newspaper tomorrow. You'll see a few love letters you might recognize.

MARIE. You don't realize what you're doing.

JEANNE. You have one week to leave France. One week. And this is not *theoretical*, this is real. It's very easy, you know, to go over to Les Halles and find some drunkard who will do anything for a bottle of cheap alcohol… and the next day he wouldn't even remember what he had done. Good night, Darling. Say hello to Poland for me.

(SLIDE: MARIE'S LIVING ROOM)

(MARIE *is seated, trembling.* **ÉMILE** *and* **MARGUERITE** *are with her.)*

ÉMILE. *(to* **MARIE***)* We could have her arrested for this, you know.

MARIE. No, let it go.

ÉMILE. This wasn't just insulting behavior. She's dangerous.

MARIE. I'm sure she's thought it out.

MARGUERITE. If this got into the press, it would just make things worse.

MARIE. By several orders of magnitude.

MARGUERITE. You're still trembling.

ÉMILE. Do you have any brandy?

MARIE. I don't think that really works. *(beat)* There's some in the cabinet.

*(***ÉMILE** *goes off to get brandy.)*

MARGUERITE. Maybe you should go away for a while. Take your girls and go on a little vacation.

MARIE. *(shrugging)* What's the use?

MARGUERITE. You need to get yourself out of danger. I wish you weren't so stubborn.

(Sound: in the street – angry voices, harsh words)

(ÉMILE *returns.*)

MARGUERITE. *(cont.)* What's that?

ÉMILE. There's a crowd out there.

MARGUERITE. A crowd...what do you mean?

ÉMILE. People. Milling around. I'm going to talk to them.

MARGUERITE. Émile, don't go out there. They sound like they're drunk.

ÉMILE. This is her private home!

(ÉMILE *exits.*)

MARGUERITE. I can't make out what they're saying.

MARIE. I can. "The Polish whore...Get the Polish whore *out.*" God, how did it get to this?

(Sound: the crowd begins to quiet down)

MARGUERITE. These are ignorant people. Don't take them seriously.

MARIE. I broke a rule. I can't pretend I didn't. It's like breaking a law of nature. You step out of a window... you fall.

MARGUERITE. You fell in love. It's not a crime. Ignore them.

MARIE. *(shrugging)* I'm already out the window.

MARGUERITE. Let me ask you something. Don't be angry.

MARIE. What?

MARGUERITE. What if you left him?

MARIE. How can I leave him?

MARGUERITE. So, is there some way can you stay with him?

MARIE. No. Obviously. I can't.

MARGUERITE. So, what will you do?

MARIE. *(shrugging)* I'm out the window.

MARGUERITE. You're not out any window! Stop that.

(ÉMILE *enters.*)

ÉMILE. I tried to talk to them. They won't leave.

MARIE. This is crazy. We have children in here.

(Sound: The crowd flares up. The thump of a stone against the house.)

MARGUERITE. What was that?

MARIE. Someone threw a stone.

ÉMILE. This is outrageous.

(Sound: a window breaking)

MARIE. We have to get the children out of here!

MARGUERITE. You wake them up and dress them. Émile and I can pack up their things.

(SLIDE: THE BOREL HOUSE)

(Sound: faint early morning birdsong)

Listen to those birds. As soon as it's light, they sing. Yesterday never happened for them.

ÉMILE. The secret to happiness is a bad memory.

MARIE. I've kept you up a long time. You've been very loving tonight. *(beat)* You know, I heard you on the telephone... Defending me to your friends.

(When they don't respond:)

I'm so sorry I put you through this.

MARGUERITE. We love you, Marie.

(Sound: a knock at the door.)

Who's that? Look through the window before you open the door. Who would be coming here at this hour?

ÉMILE. *(looking out a window)* It's Paul.

MARGUERITE. Do you want to see him?

MARIE. I have to tell him. We can't go on like this. We have to end it. It's over.

(ÉMILE exits and re-enters with PAUL.)

PAUL. *(to ÉMILE)* I thought you might be up early.

ÉMILE. I've been up since early yesterday.

We should get some sleep. I have a lecture in three hours.

(*ÉMILE and* MARGUERITE *exit.*)

PAUL. Émile called me last night, but I couldn't leave the house until now. Are the girls all right?

MARIE. They're fine. Paul, we have to…

(MARIE *turns and sees him for the first time. Despite herself,* MARIE *rushes to* PAUL *and embraces him.*)

What are you going to do between classes?

PAUL. Today?

MARIE. What if I met you at our place?

PAUL. We can't. It's too dangerous.

MARIE. No, you're right. How will you spend the day?

PAUL. I'll keep busy. See a few people.

MARIE. Who are you seeing?

PAUL. I don't know, I'll just drop in on a few friends.

MARIE. (*looking him in the eye*) Are you keeping something from me?

PAUL. No. Why would I keep anything from you?

MARIE. I feel like I'm interrogating you. Never mind. I don't want to know. You look exhausted. I suppose she told you the letters will be in the newspapers this morning.

PAUL. She took great pleasure in telling me.

MARIE. I'm not going to read it. I can't even look at a newspaper anymore. Have you stopped reading them?

PAUL. No. I keep looking for an apology from Terbougie. I've been wasting my time.

MARIE. He's a fool. Ignore him.

PAUL. It's not that easy. "You will not succeed in hiding this man in your skirts. He is nothing but a boor and a coward."

MARIE. You know it by heart.

PAUL. It's the ultimate insult. It was a deliberate challenge.

MARIE. (*slightly worried*) What if it was, what does that matter? What matters is how you take it.

PAUL. It's there in print. It won't go away. He knew exactly what he was doing.

MARIE. What does it matter what he said in a newspaper? *(beat)* Where are you going today? Please don't lie to me.

PAUL. *(after a pause)* I'm going to look for *seconds.*

MARIE. Oh, my God, no.

PAUL. I know how ridiculous it is, but I don't have a choice. I have to do it.

MARIE. Are you crazy? A duel? You're going to duel with him? You'll be killed.

PAUL. That's not certain.

MARIE. You made me want to live again, and now what? You'd risk my losing you over *this?*

PAUL. I can't let it pass. And I intend to live.

MARIE. And what if you *do* live? You think this can possibly be a secret? The press will be filled with stories of my lover dueling over me. It's disgusting.

PAUL. But it will only be something in a newspaper. Won't it?

MARIE. Paul, please. How can you do this?

PAUL. I suppose it has something to do with honor.

MARIE. It has nothing to do with honor. Any man with the slightest amount of honor who saw two people pointing pistols at each other would call the police. This is an ancient, dead game you're playing.

PAUL. Do you want me to list the duels we've had in Paris in the last ten years? It is it not an unusual event. In fact, not to respond would be entirely out of place.

MARIE. What do you care about being out of place? You're happy to go against conventional thinking as a scientist. But you can't refuse to duel over an obscure slight?

PAUL. I'm sorry. I don't see it that way.

(PAUL turns to go.)

MARIE. Paul, don't! Don't!

(SLIDE: THE BOIS DE VINCENNES)

(PAUL, TERBOUGIE and two SECONDS [the actors playing ÉMILE and PIERRE] have assembled. PAUL speaks to the audience.)

PAUL. We meet in the Bois de Vincennes. It's a cool morning with a slight mist hanging over the trees. There's Terbougie, wearing a self-satisfied smirk. *(surprised)* Across the clearing, where the ground rises, are dozens of people, watching.

Our seconds pace off the distance between us.

(The SECONDS pace off the distance between the duelists. PAUL and TERBOUGIE take their places.)

We receive our pistols and turn sideways to reduce the area of our bodies exposed to our opponent's weapon. The thought dances across my mind that in a few seconds there's an even chance I'll be dead. The same chance as flipping a coin, or pulling a black card from a deck. What am I doing here? How has everything I've worked for all my life come to hang on this one moment?

A SECOND *(actor playing ÉMILE)*. Gentlemen: Fire when ready!

PAUL. I raise my pistol, but for some reason, Terbougie doesn't raise his. *(beat)* I can't fire at him if he doesn't raise his pistol.

TERBOUGIE. My defense of Mrs. Langevin does not require me to kill her husband. I have no desire to deprive France of a precious brain.

(We see the flash of cameras recording the event.)

(SLIDE: THE FRONT PAGE OF A NEWSPAPER, showing PAUL with his pistol, looking a little shocked)

(SLIDE: LANGEVIN LIVING ROOM)

(PAUL enters.)

JEANNE. Well, how is France's precious brain today?

PAUL. I would prefer not to talk about that.

JEANNE. What a degrading circus – and with an incredibly large audience.

PAUL. The presence of reporters was a complete surprise to me.

JEANNE. Everything is a surprise to you. I suppose it surprises you that you've humiliated me again.

PAUL. This had nothing to do with you.

JEANNE. No? Then why am I ashamed to go out of the house? You never cared how you made me look. But this! This is... *(choking back emotion)* It's too much, Paul. You've worn me out. I can't take any more of this.

PAUL. Then, just give it up, Jeanne. You won't gain anything. You'll lose as much as I will. Why don't we just end it?

JEANNE. End it. Just like that. Really.

PAUL. What you want? Tell me. Do you want me back?

JEANNE. To do what with?

PAUL. Don't you realize what a trial would do to the children?

JEANNE. Is that something else that just occurred to you? Your children?

PAUL. Goddamn it! Don't be such a pig about this.

JEANNE. Pig. Very nice.

PAUL. You know what else would come out at a trial? Besides the letters? You're a woman who has physically abused her husband. People have seen me come to the lab with black and blue marks on my face. You want them to testify? You think you'll still be the poor, long suffering victim after that?

JEANNE. You would debase yourself that much for her. You'd parade into court as the weakling husband who lets his wife throw him around the house. All for her.

PAUL. Let them finally see what I'm married to.

JEANNE. Yes, you'd love that. "Oh, of course he betrayed her – she was cruel to him." Well, I'm sorry, you won't get the satisfaction. There's not going to be any trial.

PAUL. All right, then. Good.

JEANNE. But I'll get everything else I want.

PAUL. What do you want?

JEANNE. You will admit what you did was a disgrace. In writing.

PAUL. Yes, fine. And you'll stop making these insane murder threats.

JEANNE. Oh, all right. After all, a human life is worth something. Let's say eight hundred francs a month.

(PAUL shakes his head in disbelief.)

PAUL. Don't be absurd. What about the children?

JEANNE. Eight hundred francs.

PAUL. *Fine.* What about the children?

JEANNE. I'll have full custody.

PAUL. No.

JEANNE. You can have lunch with them occasionally.

PAUL. No.

JEANNE. Well, we'll work something out.

PAUL. When? We'll work something out when?

JEANNE. As time goes on. We don't have to decide right now. We have our whole lives ahead of us.

(As she smiles serenely...)

(SLIDE: MARIE'S NEW LAB)

(MARIE is on the telephone.)

MARIE. *(to the operator)* Yes, I'm calling Professor H. R. Törnebladh in Stockholm, Sweden... TÖRNEBLADH. The number there is... *(reading from the telegram)* 463-626. All right, I'll wait for you to call back. *(hanging up)*

(PAUL enters.)

So, did you have a nice duel?

PAUL. I think we can resolve all this. Jeanne and I finally have a settlement.

MARIE. *(not very interested)* Really?

PAUL. She and I will share time with the children and there will be no trial.

MARIE. No trial...?

PAUL. I got her to see how damaging a trial would be for both of us.

MARIE. Now there won't be a trial? I *want* a trial.

PAUL. Why? I can't let you go through that.

MARIE. You can't *let* me? Listen to this. *(holding out a telegram)* It came in after you were out playing in the park. This is from Törnebladh in Stockholm. *(reading)* "The ridiculous duel of Mr. Langevin gives the impression that the letters in the press were in fact written by you. Please telephone me and indicate that you will not accept the Nobel Prize until the Langevin trial has shown that there is no foundation to these accusations." *(looking at PAUL)* They want me to stay away from Stockholm until a trial clears my name – but you can't *let* me go through a trial?

PAUL. There's no way to know how a trial would turn out. It could go completely against you.

MARIE. That's right. It's a little like a duel.

PAUL. Marie...she'll take away my children. They're gifted, they're curious. They let me teach them. Jeanne would just let their brains rot.

MARIE. *(after a beat)* Your children. No, I understand. Tell her you accept the offer.

PAUL. Please forgive me.

MARIE. It's ironic. That's one of the first things that attracted me to you. The feelings you had for your children. How did I go from that to putting my own children second? I must have been out of my head...

(MARIE rises, but stops, supporting herself on the edge of her chair.)

PAUL. Are you all right?

MARIE. I'm fine...actually...I'm...I'm actually...

PAUL. Can I get you something?

MARIE. I'm all right. Goodbye, Paul.

PAUL. You want me to leave?

MARIE. No, I mean goodbye.

PAUL. What do you mean, "goodbye?" You mean forever..?

MARIE. In the sense that we'll never touch each other again, I suppose I do.

PAUL. Is that what you want?

MARIE. What I want? I want to live with you, work with you, talk all through the night with you, go to the country in the summer, walk in the woods, raise my children with you. Reality, as it turns out, is something else.

PAUL. I can't accept this. I won't.

MARIE. It's just reality, Paul.

PAUL. You said I made you want to live.

MARIE. Yes, well, it turns out that wanting to live isn't something I can get from you or from the committee in Stockholm, or anyone else. You know what this is? When we saw that first little glow of radiation, we didn't know where it came from. We thought the radium was being activated by some outside source of energy. Sunlight, or something. But we were wrong. This is just like that. Existence isn't reflected light. It comes from inside the atom.

PAUL. Marie…isn't there some…

MARIE. Please, Paul.

PAUL. I won't lose you as a friend…?

MARIE. No, that's not possible.

PAUL. *(after a beat)* I suppose I should go.

(He moves to kiss her.)

MARIE. *(holding back from his kiss)* I don't think so. No.

PAUL. Will you call me if you…if you need anything?

MARIE. I think I'm going to have to do this alone.

*(**PAUL** nods. He starts to leave, but turns back.)*

PAUL. You've got to put some distance between you and the radium.

MARIE. Please…

PAUL. It's going to kill you.

MARIE. I'm suffering from exhaustion.

PAUL. Why did Pierre fall in the street? It wasn't the radiation? What else could it have been?

MARIE. It was raining.

PAUL. God, you don't *want* to know, do you?

MARIE. Paul…what I think you ought to do is…just go.

(Sound: The phone begins to ring.)

PAUL. Yes. *(beat)* Yes.

(PAUL exits. MARIE picks up the phone.)

MARIE. Doctor Törnebladh? I have your telegram. I think if I did what you're asking me to do, it would be a very grave mistake…yes… *(listening)* Because the prize is being awarded for the discovery of radium and polonium, not for anything in my private life. The work, not the person…Well, I'm sorry you don't agree. I'm saddened, actually…No, I'm *not* feeling very well – thank you for asking…Yes, it's a *very* long trip. *(slight beat)* But, I will not turn down the prize, and I *will* come to Stockholm. Goodbye, Doctor Törnebladh.

(Sound: a train)

(VIDEO: THE COUNTRYSIDE WHIZZING BY ON THE WAY FROM PARIS TO STOCKHOLM IN DECEMBER)

TERBOUGIE. This foreign woman claims to speak in the name of reason, which is hideously unfeminine, She scorns French tradition. She is simply a foreign, intellectual, emancipated woman of the worst kind. And, as everyone is well aware, Mrs. Curie's scientific exploits are vastly over-rated. She had never done anything in physics before her marriage…has she ever done *anything…alone?*

(SLIDE: THE NOBEL HALL, SWEDEN.)

(MARIE crosses the stage. Her steps are weak and halting. MARIE reaches the podium. She's frail, but determined.)

MARIE. Distinguished guests, members of the Swedish Academy…Some 15 years ago the radiation of uranium was discovered by Henri Becquerel, and two years later the study of…*(faltering, but pulling herself together)* …the study of this phenomenon was extended to other substances, first by me, and then by Pierre Curie and myself. Isolating radium as a pure salt… *was done by me alone…*The isolation of radium has furnished proof of my hypothesis that radioactivity is an atomic property of matter…We have here an entirely separate kind of chemistry…which we might well call the chemistry of the invisible.

*(**MARIE** moves downstage, joined the cast.)*

(to the audience) Really, how can you not step into the mystery? The universe is a fascinating place, isn't it? Full of riddles: radioactivity that can prolong life and end it. Puzzling, maddening riddles. But, how can you not step into the mystery?

*(**PIERRE** hands **MARIE** a small box containing a vial of radium. **MARIE** holds up the vial, fascinated by its hypnotic glow.)*

MARIE. *(cont.)* It's beautiful, isn't it? If you have enough of it, you can actually read by it.

(The lights fade to black.)

END OF PLAY.

OTHER TITLES AVAILABLE FROM SAMUEL FRENCH

EMILIE'S VOLTAIRE
Arthur Giron

Dramatic Comedy / 1m, 1f / Simple Set

Emilie's Voltaire is a passionate dramatic comedy that explores a love affair that scandalized all of Europe between Voltaire, the greatest wit of his time, and the beautiful scientist Emilie du Chatelet. It takes place before the French Revolution.

Winner! Galileo Prize for Playwriting

"What happens when the minds of two seekers of knowledge, one a challenger of life and the other a hedonistic rule breaker, meet? The result is a tumultuous, fascinating 16-year love affair that is wonderfully portrayed in Arthur Giron's *Emilie's Voltaire*...The captivating *Emilie's Voltaire* is an inside look at genius and the underlying emotions that feed it. Definitely a bit of history you're pleased to discover." – *OffBroadway.com*

"The intellectual, emotional and sexual sparks fly...an unusual and fascinating play." – William Wolf, *Wolf Entertainment Guide*

"Arthur Giron's words are what actors long to wrap their voices around." – *The New York Examiner*

"A beautiful pas de deux of dialogue!" – *MusicOMH*